BENJI, THE BAD DAY, AND ME

by Sally J. Pla

illustrated by Ken Min

Radar-1

Lee & Low Books Inc.
New York

Text copyright © 2018 by Sally J. Pla
Illustrations copyright © 2018 by Ken Min
LEE & LOW BOOKS Inc., 95 Madison Avenue, New York, NY 10016
leeandlow.com
Edited by Jessica V. Echeverria
Designed by Kimi Weart
Production by The Kids at Our House
The text is set in Museo
The illustrations are rendered in acrylic and colored pencil, and digitally enhanced
Manufactured in Malaysia by Tien Wah Press
10 9 8 7 6 5 4 3 2 1
First Edition

Library of Congress Cataloging-in-Publication Data
Names: Pla, Sally J., author. | Min, Ken, illustrator.
Title: Benji, the bad day, and me / by Sally J. Pla; illustrated by Ken Min.
Description: First edition. | New York: Lee & Low Books Inc., [2018] |
Summary: Sammy is having a very bad day at school and at home until his
autistic brother, Benji, finds a way to make him feel better.
Identifiers: LCCN 2018004063 | ISBN 9781620143452 (hardcover: alk. paper)
Subjects: | CYAC: Brothers—Fiction. | Mood (Psychology)—Fiction. |
Autism—Fiction. | Family life—Fiction.
Classification: LCC PZ7.1.P6213 Ben 2018 | DDC [E]—dc23
LC record available at https://lccn.loc.gov/2018004063

For my boys—and for everyone who's ever had a bad day

—*S.J.P.*

For Mark and Mary—my "brother" and "sister" who look after me

—*K.M.*

At recess, I got yelled at for kicking the fence. At lunch, they ran out of my favorite pizza, so I didn't eat. And on the bus home, the driver missed my stop, so I had to walk all the way back in the rain.

Now I'm hungry, cold, and wet.

Grrrrrrrrrrrrrrrr!

"*Shhhhhhhhhh,*" says Mama as soon as I open the door. "Benji's playing in his box."

When Benji's in his box, it's because he's had a bad day at preschool. When Benji's had a bad day, we tiptoe and speak softly.

When I've had a bad day, no one tiptoes or speaks softly.

Benji, Mama, and I made that box last summer. Mama cut the window flaps, and Benji and I splashed on the paint. Inside, it's cozy and safe, but only big enough for Benji and his blue blanket.

I sure wish *I* had a box for days like this.

Benji wiggles his fingers at me.
"Hi, Benji," I say softly.

Benji's face appears. "Wet Sammy,"
Benji says.

"Samuel!" says Mama. "There's water all over the floor! Take your shoes off this instant."

It's not *my* fault I had to walk all that way in the rain.

Benji's block city is spread all around. "Watch your step!" Mama says. "Benji's been working hard on that."

"I know. I helped!" I start to say—but Mama's phone rings, and she turns away.

I stick my tongue out at the box. I do my best karate kick high in the air, above Benji's block city.

I've always wanted to learn karate. Mama says I can't right now because the classes are on Tuesdays, and that's when we have to visit the Super-Happy Lady at Benji's clinic downtown.

"Let's bounce the ball!" Super-Happy Lady likes to say. But Benji never does.

"Let's play a game!" But Benji never plays.

Meanwhile, I'm told to sit in the waiting room and *not bother anyone*.

On Super-Happy Lady days, we always get back home tired. So Mama will make berry smoothies to help us feel better. Then she'll wrap Benji tight in his big blue blanket, just how he likes, and tell him, "You're my little burrito!"

But today there are no berry smoothies and no burritos. Today
Mama is busy and Benji is hiding. This day is just plain old rotten.

Thump! goes the box. It's Benji, kicking around in there.

"Hey!" I say. "Come out and I'll teach you karate!"

But he doesn't.

So I go to the kitchen and pour some cereal. But when I add the milk, too much gushes out. I am grumpy, hungry, and cold, and now there is *milk everywhere*!

I have had it with this fence-kicking, rain-dripping, milk-spilling day. I cry mad-sad shivery tears.

No one notices.

Ka-thunk! Benji's coming out!

He holds his blanket up high and tiptoes
through the block city.

Benji spreads his blanket flat on the floor. What's he doing?

He pulls me down on the fuzzy blueness and makes me lie straight and still. Then he rolls me over and over. He works hard to wrap me up tight.

Benji leans over me. His forehead clunks my forehead. His eyes look right in my eyes.

"You're my little burrito," he says.

I open the blanket and let Benji in.
"You're my little brother!" I say.

And that's how Mama finds us.

"Can I come in too?" she asks.

Whether the day is good or bad, Benji and I will be okay. That's because the two of us are brothers.

Side by side is where we are, and how we'll always be!

AUTHOR'S NOTE

At our house, our autistic and non-autistic sons alike had fuzzy blankets they carried around, and they often asked—on both good days and bad—to be "wrapped tight into burritos." This can be comfy and calming. And it's what sparked the idea for this story.

It's important to note that no two autistic kids are alike, and their needs and behaviors will be different. Some, like Benji, are supersensitive to sensory input—the world can feel too bright, too loud, and too intense. Other kids are sensory seekers. Some may like to drum on things and clap their hands and shout out. And many kids like to "stim," to rhythmically fidget or move as a way to disperse extra energy and stress.

Certain autistic kids will visit a sensory gym or OT (occupational therapy) clinic, as in the Super-Happy Lady illustration, to help with coordination and sensory processing. But not all. Different kids have different needs, strengths, and challenges.

It's not always easy being a brother or a sister. It's hard, at times, to be patient. We all have bad days, and it's okay to express those feelings in appropriate ways. Despite the bad days, though, sibling bonds can be one of life's best and most important gifts.

Thank you for reading about Sammy and Benji!